Wendy J Hall
Visit the website at
https://www.mediwonderland.com/

First Printing: March 2018
Mediwonderland

ISBN-13: 978-1985332034

<u>DEDICATION</u>

To Riley James, who continues to have a helpful and loving spirit despite the challenges he and others with Albinism have.

Kylie's Eye Check

medi
wonderland

Wendy J. Hall

Kylie kept on falling over and couldn't see what her teacher was writing on the board.

The worse thing was that it was getting worse. The letters were all blurry and the teacher thought she was not paying attention. She told her mom.

"Your health check with Dr. Daniel is next week, and he'll check your eyes. We can see what the results are."

They went for a check-up every year to make sure Kylie was healthy.

The last check was in a small room. There were lots of posters with black letters on them. Kylie had to hold something like a big spoon over each eye and say the letter. But she could only see lots of blurry black lines.

The technician wrote something in her record book and said she could go back to her mom.

Then they went to wait outside Dr. Daniel's office for their turn to see him, to find out if she was growing up properly. Soon, they were sitting at his desk waiting to hear.

"Everything looks good, but I'm worried about your eyes. Have you been having problems seeing things?"

Kylie nodded sadly, and a tear ran down her cheek.

"Don't worry, Kylie. I'll refer you to a special place called 'The Children's Eye Center.' You'll see an ophthalmologist, a special doctor who knows all about how eyes work and has lots of machines there to check you over."

The next day, Kylie and her mom went to the center.

Kylie looked around and felt scared. She could see lots of rooms filled with very scary-looking machines.

She sat sadly on the sofa in the waiting area. Then she heard someone say, "Hi. My name's Riley. What's yours?"

"My name's Kylie," she answered in a very quiet voice.

She noticed that his skin, hair and eyes were very white and he looked different.

He saw her looking and said, "I have a condition called Albinism. We don't have something called 'pigment,' which gives us color. Albinism affects our eyes especially badly and at first they thought I was blind. I had to come to places like this a lot and I found it really scary. Can you see the special things I have on my eyes called lenses? I still can't see clearly, but they help a lot.

"Let's talk about today. It'll be like going on a tour through different rooms, which they sometimes call labs. Would you like me to tell you about some of them?"

"Yes, please."

"Don't worry about the long names of the machines."

"They look like evil monsters," said Kylie. "Is it going to hurt?"

"No," said Riley. "I must tell you though, that there's a test you won't like, but I'll leave it till the end.

"Each machine gives information to the ophthalmologist and he or she will be able to help you see better, and that's a good thing, right?"

Kylie nodded and sheepishly said, "I guess so."

"Our eyes have lots of parts that all do different jobs and they'll check them.

"For some tests, you'll need to sit very close to the machine and put your chin on a special place.

Human Eye

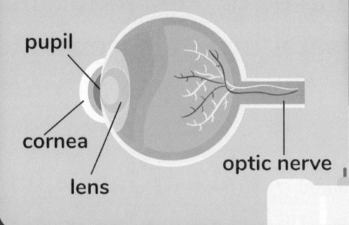

pupil

cornea

lens

optic nerve

"Then, you'll have to do different things. It does feel a little bit weird at first.

"You'll go into the rooms or labs and do lots of tests. The coolest room is one where you'll need to have tests with lights.

"At first, I hated that room because it's dark. The machines in there are called 'ocular' machines. The reason it's dark is that they need to see how your eyes move and they need to use lights to do that."

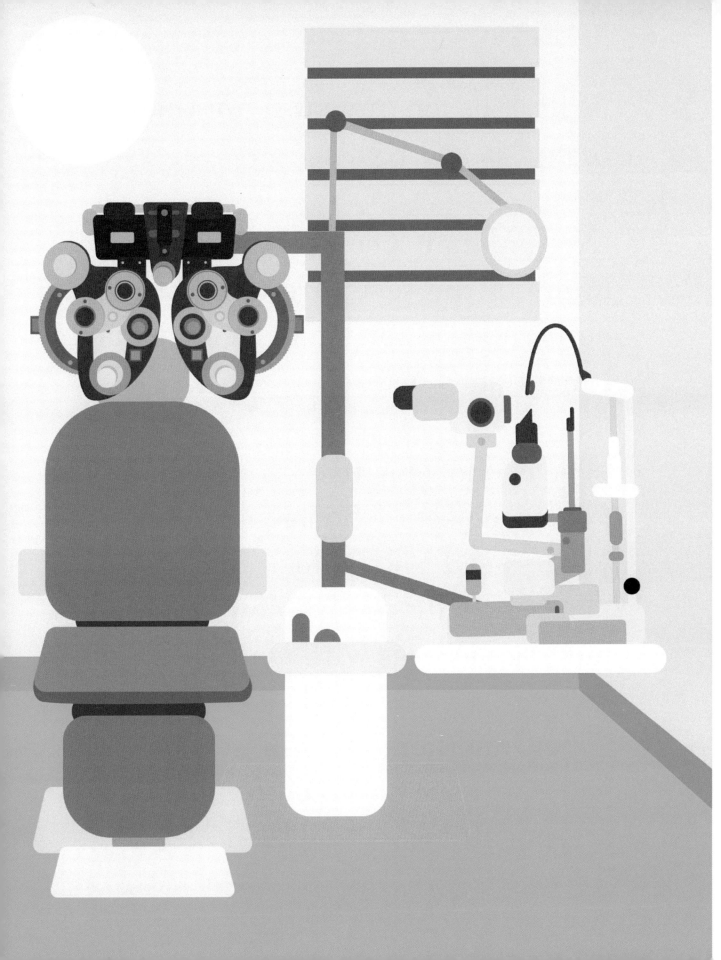

"Will I be on my own in that dark room?" asked Kylie.

"No, special people will help you. Many of the tests are ones I have to do because I don't have that pigment I mentioned before.

"They'll do one test to see how you follow objects. Someone may hold your head straight and then a machine will record how you follow moving pictures with your eyes.

"Then another one will see how well you can gaze at something, just like staring at it.

"There are many other machines you'll visit today, because it's your first time and there are so many eye illnesses it would take me a day to tell you about all of them.

"I'll tell you about two of the most important tests. One tests how well you can see from the outer part of your eyes.

"You'll sit at a machine and every time you see a light, you press a button. It's kind of like a video game!

"Now, I need to tell you about the part you won't like today. I didn't like it at all.

"The nurse will put special eye drops into your eyes, then you sit and wait. Your eyes will go blurry. The drops make the black circle in your eye get bigger or 'dilate,' as they say. It lets the ophthalmologist look right into the back of your eyes at something called your retina. The retina is very important because it sends messages to your brain.

"The specialist will wear funny things like binoculars but might stick something on your eye and it won't feel good and will make tears come out of your eyes. Just try to think of nice things.

"At some stage, you'll do lots of tests with colors and letters. Then at the end they'll see how they can help you with special glasses or lenses like the ones I'm wearing."

Just at that moment, Kylie heard her name. It was her turn.

She looked at Riley and said, "Thank you so much for helping me. I will be brave because of you. I didn't expect to make a new friend."

"Me too," said Riley. "I know it's hard but they **will** help you. We'll meet again soon."

Kylie said goodbye as she was led into the first room but she was smiling!

About the Author

Originally from the UK, Wendy speaks five languages and has authored over 100 educational books. The inspiration for this innovative series comes from personal experience: Her own daughter, then aged eight, once spent a year in hospital and underwent major surgery.

While taking care of a scared child, Wendy could not find materials that helped her navigate the healthcare system. This situation kindled a dream: to provide parents and medical professionals with a tool to make medical procedures, illnesses, and adverse childhood circumstances less frightening.

Wendy has extensive knowledge of the medical field as she herself suffers from a rare, chronic illness. An award-winning Patient Leader, she works to improve healthcare by advocating and educating.

To learn more about Wendy, please visit the website:

https://www.mediwonderland.com

Made in the USA
Monee, IL
14 September 2019